THIS STICKER BOOK BELONGS TO

MY FAVORITE STICKER

MY FAVORITE STICKER

MY FAVORITE STICKER

MY FAVORITE STICKER

MY FAVORITE STICKER

MY FAVORITE STICKER

MY FAVORITE STICKER

MY FAVORITE STICKER

MY FAVORITE STICKER

MY FAVORITE STICKER

MY FAVORITE STICKER

MY FAVORITE STICKER

MY FAVORITE STICKER

MY FAVORITE STICKER

MY FAVORITE STICKER

MY FAVORITE STICKER

MY FAVORITE STICKER

MY FAVORITE STICKER

MY FAVORITE STICKER

MY FAVORITE STICKER

MY FAVORITE STICKER

MY FAVORITE STICKER

MY FAVORITE STICKER

MY FAVORITE STICKER

MY FAVORITE STICKER

MY FAVORITE STICKER

MY FAVORITE STICKER

MY FAVORITE STICKER

MY FAVORITE STICKER

MY FAVORITE STICKER

MY FAVORITE STICKER

MY FAVORITE STICKER

MY FAVORITE STICKER

MY FAVORITE STICKER

MY FAVORITE STICKER

MY FAVORITE STICKER

MY FAVORITE STICKER

MY FAVORITE STICKER

MY FAVORITE STICKER

MY FAVORITE STICKER

MY FAVORITE STICKER

MY FAVORITE STICKER

MY FAVORITE STICKER

MY FAVORITE STICKER

MY FAVORITE STICKER

MY FAVORITE STICKER

MY FAVORITE STICKER

MY FAVORITE STICKER

MY FAVORITE STICKER

MY FAVORITE STICKER

MY FAVORITE STICKER

MY FAVORITE STICKER

MY FAVORITE STICKER

MY FAVORITE STICKER

MY FAVORITE STICKER

MY FAVORITE STICKER

MY FAVORITE STICKER

MY FAVORITE STICKER

MY FAVORITE STICKER

MY FAVORITE STICKER

MY FAVORITE STICKER

MY FAVORITE STICKER

MY FAVORITE STICKER

MY FAVORITE STICKER

MY FAVORITE STICKER

MY FAVORITE STICKER

MY FAVORITE STICKER

MY FAVORITE STICKER

MY FAVORITE STICKER

MY FAVORITE STICKER

MY FAVORITE STICKER

MY FAVORITE STICKER

MY FAVORITE STICKER

MY FAVORITE STICKER

MY FAVORITE STICKER

MY FAVORITE STICKER

MY FAVORITE STICKER

MY FAVORITE STICKER

MY FAVORITE STICKER

MY FAVORITE STICKER

MY FAVORITE STICKER

MY FAVORITE STICKER

MY FAVORITE STICKER

MY FAVORITE STICKER

MY FAVORITE STICKER

MY FAVORITE STICKER

MY FAVORITE STICKER

MY FAVORITE STICKER

MY FAVORITE STICKER

MY FAVORITE STICKER

MY FAVORITE STICKER

MY FAVORITE STICKER

MY FAVORITE STICKER

MY FAVORITE STICKER

MY FAVORITE STICKER

MY FAVORITE STICKER

MY FAVORITE STICKER

MY FAVORITE STICKER

MY FAVORITE STICKER

MY FAVORITE STICKER

MY FAVORITE STICKER

MY FAVORITE STICKER

MY FAVORITE STICKER

MY FAVORITE STICKER

MY FAVORITE STICKER

MY FAVORITE STICKER

MY FAVORITE STICKER

MY FAVORITE STICKER

Made in the USA
Las Vegas, NV
29 November 2023